Uneasy Listening

A caricature guide to
20th-century Composers
by John Minnion

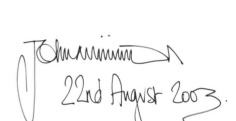

John Minnion
22nd August 2003.

CHECKMATE BOOKS

65 Dudlow Lane Liverpool L18 2EY
Telephone: +44 (0)151 8950
www.checkmatebooks.com

"Nowadays we composers feel like the
mustard at the great feast of music"
— *Witold Lutoslawski*

CW00584852

Published 2003 by

Checkmate Books

65 Dudlow Lane, Liverpool L18 2EY
Telephone +44 (0)151-722 8950
contact@checkmatebooks.com

www.checkmatebooks.com

Printed by Page Bros (Norwich) Ltd

ISBN 0-9544499-1-6

Re-use of pictures:
Enquiries should be made to
contact@checkmatebooks.com

FOREWORD BY ROBERT SAXTON

John Minnion's pictures of composers are, in the best sense, 'classic' caricatures, at once capturing a victim's essential visual features and basic personality traits. For example, his drawing of my former teacher, Elisabeth Lutyens (see p.71) delineates both her slightly cross expression and incessant worrying, while presenting us with an image of an infinitely wise bird. It is a masterpiece of expressive economy and draughtsmanship. I have the original on my study wall, from where it looks at me, hopefully acting as a reminder of the standards demanded thirty years ago when I was a student. Elisabeth never charged for more than an hour's tuition, but lessons frequently lasted four or five hours, followed by supper on a tray in front of the television. Her integrity, generosity, care and humanity are qualities which I miss even today.

Beneath the picture of Elisabeth hangs a caricature of me (see p.104). My partner, Teresa Cahill, secretly sought out John Minnion some years ago and bought both as a surprise present. Perhaps unpredictably, I found my 'portrait' comforting from the moment I saw it; my appearance and manner as represented sum up exactly how I feel when lecturing or teaching, which is what I assume I am doing in the picture. It is uncanny that someone whom I have never met, who draws only from photographs, can portray me in what is a public situation, and yet bring to the fore aspects of my character which I presumed remain hidden in public.

In the pictures and text contained in this book, John Minnion displays his profound care for 20th Century music and its creators, broaching the issue of the composer and his/her public at large. With its acute and brilliant verbal summaries acting as a counterpart to the wit and stylish individuality of the drawings, his collection will, I am certain, come to be seen as an important chronicle of its era, becoming part of the canon of great political and artistic caricatures which have not merely entertained, but made us think deeply for nearly three centuries about our entire cultural heritage and its values.

John writes about the communication problems between composers and listeners at the end of the 20th Century. He asked me what it is like to be a composer today. I do sense the past strongly as a living force and I have instinctively embraced concepts and technical achievements of those who have paved the way. Schoenberg said that he was proud to have learned from Mozart and (without making comparisons!) I say the same of myself in relation to Schoenberg. As to accessibility, of course I want to communicate with my fellow human beings but, as I've said many times (both verbally and in print), I will not do so at any price. I have always written music (or tried to!); it is something I do, just as physicists engage in physics. The difficult and great art of writing music does not change fundamentally; the social situation and external demands may alter, but 'being a composer today' is, for me, simply the pleasure of writing notes on paper.

Robert Saxton 16-2-03

SEVERE CLASSICAL FINN MEETS ALL-EMBRACING ROMANTIC JEW

Walking with Mahler in the Finnish forests, Sibelius enthused about the essence of a good symphony: the severity of form and the interconnectedness between motifs. 'No, no', responded Mahler, 'The symphony must be like the world – it must contain everything'. There was much talk throughout the century of the death of the symphony. How could this supreme example of narrative music survive a new age of music that was abandoning the mechanisms of forward movement: melody, cadence and key?

*Even so, both these 20th Century composers achieved monuments in symphonic history, each on his own terms. No symphonist has matched the concentration of content in Sibelius's **Seventh Symphony**, nor the comprehensiveness of Mahler's **Eighth Symphony**.*

(right) Sibelius

The 19th Century was the Age of Romanticism in Europe, and as it drew to a close music had become overblown and confessional. Tchaikovsky's **Pathétique Symphony** (1893), for instance, told such a story of private despair that the only decent follow-up was suicide. Egos had become so inflated that Wagner's **Ring** was not so much an opera as a religious festival, demanding pilgrimage to a specially built concert hall in Bayreuth.

In Vienna, the capital of the *fin de siècle* musical world, maestro Gustav Mahler ruled the Opera House and spent his summer holidays writing gigantic symphonies for huge orchestras, often with solo singers and choruses on and off stage. In Munich, Richard Strauss (aged 35) had written **Ein Heldenleben**, (*The Hero's Life*), a tone-poem starring himself and quoting from many of his previous hits.

In Russia, Scriabin had come to believe he was some kind of deity and was planning **Mysterium**: a multi-media extravaganza featuring orchestras, choruses, dancers, perfume and an organ that would produce colours instead of notes. Unfortunately he died of a septic boil on the lip before the event could come to pass.

In England things were more measured, though the scale was still large. Oratorio was the most popular musical event, performed with vast forces in packed houses. The piece of the moment was **Hiawatha's Wedding Feast** by Coleridge-Taylor, and a great composer had arrived at last in Edward Elgar, leading an overdue English musical renaissance with noble music that reflected the self-confidence of the Empire.

The Romantic bubble was about to burst, along with a few other bubbles. For a start, with expression becoming so personal the strain on musical syntax was becoming intolerable. Sonata form was barely adequate for these bloated new programmes and the boundaries of harmony were being stretched as composers came up with their personal new chords. The tonal system, based on major and minor scales

FALL OF THE ROMANTIC EMPIRE

that had served music since Renaissance times, had never been quite the same since Wagner and was beginning to break up. Atonalism beckoned.

There were also new influences from other cultures. Delius heard the singing of black plantation workers in Florida, early stirrings of the truly 20th Century idiom of jazz. Nationalism, a political force in the 1800s, had become cultural, and composers from Norway to the Balkans were exploring folk idioms.

Debussy had been profoundly affected by the sound of the Javanese gamelan he heard at the 1889 Paris Exhibition. To Western ears such music had no beginning, middle nor end: following it was a challenge. But Debussy was turning his back on the Austro-German tradition, and most significantly on the symphonic form of development that moved towards a conclusion. His music in pieces like his nocturne **Nuages** (1899) was not a forward moving narrative but a landscape of colours, textures and shadows. This 'Impressionism' was a new approach requiring innovations in harmony and orchestration. To liberate himself from the cadences that had been the mainstay of forward movement, he experimented with different modes such as the wholetone and pentatonic scales.

It was Mahler whose work bridged the great change from Romanticism to Modernism, though it took several decades before it was universally recognised that his massive symphonies were more signif-

icant than a conductor's spare-time indulgencies. His **First Symphony** sounded like Tchaikovsky, but his **Ninth**, **Tenth** and **The Song of the Earth**, though still deeply romantic, looked forward to the sound-world of Schoenberg and Webern. (Though the scale could not be more different: Webern was so concise that you could fit most of his life's work inside one Mahler symphony.)

Mahler's death and World War I marked the end of Romanticism as a movement. For most of the 20th Century, romantic traits such as introspection, sentiment and nostalgia were kept at bay in classical music, and the epithet 'romantic' became a sign of disapproval.

With this bathwater a number of babies may have been thrown out. Accessibility, for a start, and, most seriously, melody. (Melody tends to be forward moving.)

Elgar and Sibelius are examples of fine 20th Century composers who retired early, partly through awareness of becoming unwanted and unfashionable. Rachmaninov confessed 'I cannot cast out the old way of writing and I cannot acquire the new', and concentrated instead on performing work he had already written which was full of yearning melody.

In fact Romanticism never went away. For good or bad it found new paths in popular music, so successfully that at the 20th Century's end it may be that classical music has lost its way without it and may never claim it back again.

1900
Puccini *Tosca*
Elgar *Dream of Gerontius*
Mahler *Symphony No.4*

1901
Elgar *Pomp and Circumstance March No.1*
Rachmaninov *Piano Concerto No.2*

Edward Elgar

1857-1934

Son of a Worcester shopkeeper who emerged into the limelight in his forties to be acclaimed England's greatest composer since Purcell. Being self-taught probably saved his oversensitive and introspective personality from being swamped by the pomp and circumstance of the Edwardian Age. Beneath its nobility his music expresses the underlying insecurities of an Empire about to collapse, as well as a personal melancholy. World War I and the death of his wife just about did for him and he composed little after his *Cello Concerto* of 1919, which stands as an elegy for the lost age.

Giacomo Puccini

1858-1924

Last in the line of Italian lyric opera composers that included Bellini and Verdi. King of the 20th Century box-office thanks to his sense of drama, gift for memorable tunes and penchant for graphic subject matter. An egotistical hypochondriac, his hobbies included sexual infidelity and duck-shooting.

1902
Debussy *Pelleas et Melisande*
Sibelius *Symphony No.2*
Nielsen *Symphony No.2*

1903
Sibelius *Violin Concerto*

1904
Puccini *Madame Butterfly*
Delius *Sea Drift*

Claude Debussy
1862-1918

Music's chief Impressionist, the French composer who broke the German monopoly, seducing music into a new sound-world for the new century. His subtle, indeterminate harmonies often used scales from other cultures. His seascape *La Mer*, which evokes in sound the interplay of light and water, was written in Eastbourne where he was holed up with his mistress hiding from scandal after his abandoned wife had attempted suicide. Poor for much of his life, he was pursued by lawsuits over debts up until his death at the end of World War I .

Frederick Delius *1862-1934*

Bradford-born composer who, after a spell growing oranges in Florida, arrived in France. Enjoyed a dissolute Parisian period sharing café life with Strindberg, Gauguin and Munch before marrying an artist and settling for the rest of his life in a village called Grez. Turning his back on other musical influences, he followed his own path, writing lyrical nature pieces with flowing, chromatic harmonies. When syphilis paralysed and blinded him, he was helped out by an amanuensis, Eric Fenby, who not only notated his music but read him the latest test match scores from England.

Gustav Mahler

1860-1911

Would have been remembered as
one of the great conductors even if
he had never composed a note. In
fact he composed a vast number of
notes: ten titanic symphonies embracing huge dramatic ideas such as
Resurrection, Redemption and
Death – in particular his own death,
which haunted him and duly
arrived when he was only 51. In his
spare time he was married to Alma,
'the most beautiful woman in
Vienna'. Her own compositions
were shelved away on his orders,
but retrieved years later after a marriage guidance session with Freud.

Richard Strauss

1864-1949

Munich-born composer of richly-orchestrated tone-poems and operas. The nearest the 20th Century got to a Mozart: an elegant melodist who was self-confident enough to ignore the fact that melody was out of fashion. His rewards were lifelong riches and fame, though he made musical enemies among modernists and political enemies because of the position he held in Hitler's Germany, stubbornly believing that Art was above politics. In his last years he wrote the *Four Last Songs*, as serene a farewell to his life and to Romanticism as could be imagined.

1907

Sibelius *Symphony No.3*
Mahler *Symphony No.8*

Carl Nielsen
1865-1931

Hardly known in his lifetime outside his native Denmark, this boy from a poor family of 14 children grew up to be a significant symphonist, developing ideas of struggle and reconciliation in musical structure. His work is unsentimental, exuberant and expansive. His Fifth Symphony represents an all-out war between Good and Evil in which the Satanic role is played by an improvising side-drum.

Jean Sibelius
1865-1957

Finland's greatest hero, a major symphonist who enjoyed wine, cigars and conversation but was austere and self-critical in his composing. He pared symphonic structure down to such extent that his *Seventh Symphony* was condensed into a single 20-minute movement. This was a hard act to follow, and an Eighth never appeared, though he lived another 26 years. To English tastes his musical language represented a 'third way', more attractive than Schoenberg or Stravinsky.

10

Granville Bantock

1868-1946

A major figure in the English musical renaissance, who did much as a conductor to promote his fellow-composers and was one of the first to draw attention outside Finland to Sibelius. Yet he himself was a disappointing composer, despite his energy and prolific output even in old age. Wrote too much too easily.

John Ireland

1879-1962

Introspective organist, choirmaster and teacher (eg. of Benjamin Britten). Composed songs and piano music in a peculiarly English lyrical style. Wrote his poignant *Violin Sonata No.2* during World War I expressing a yearning for the old world that was passing. Long outliving the age in which such sensibilities were cherished, he retired to a windmill in Sussex.

Alexander Scriabin *1872-1915*

Mystical Russian who composed dense, luxuriant pieces with titles like *Poem of Ecstasy*. Excessively egomaniacal even for a composer, he believed music was at one with colour and that he was at one with God. His impressionistic atonality, particularly in piano works, won respect from his fellow composers.

Sergei Rachmaninov
1873-1943 (right)

Shy Russian pianist with huge hands, a composer prone to reflecting his melancholia in music, like his mentor Tchaikovsky. Left Russia in 1917, settling in the USA where he wrote little, but performed and recorded his music in a way that smaller-handed pianists could only envy. His hugely popular *Piano Concerto No.2* was dedicated to his hypnotherapist.

14

Samuel Coleridge-Taylor
1875-1912

Son of an African doctor and English mother. His composing was encouraged by Elgar. Scored a huge hit in 1898 with his student cantata *Hiawatha's Wedding Feast* but never again matched that success. Visiting the USA he did much to help improve the lot of black people and incorporated Negro elements in his music. On the brink of emigrating there he died of pneumonia.

Ethel Smyth
1858-1944 (right)

Formidable daughter of military folk, whose music impressed Brahms and Tchaikovsky. A suffragette, who taught Mrs Pankhurst how to throw stones. She did time with her in Holloway Gaol, where she conducted with a toothbrush as her fellow-inmates sang her *March of the Women*. Lusted after Virginia Woolf.

SHORT CLASSICAL RUSSIAN MEETS TALL ROMANTIC RUSSIAN

Stravinsky referred to Rachmaninov as 'a six-and-a-half-foot scowl'. He had plenty to scowl about. While abandoning Romanticism was the most natural thing in the world for the classically-inclined Stravinsky it was quite impossible for Rachmaninov.
What they did share was a profound sense of loss in their exile from Russia. Stravinsky called it his greatest crisis. War and revolution led to much displacement in the 20th Century, much personal sadness but, ultimately, the cultural enrichment of America.

② HURRICANE

Romanticism had started as a reaction to Classicism in the growing belief that emotions should be expressed in art and that the classical rules and restraints were preventing this. Romantics believed the individual imagination to be paramount even when it defied reason. The curious thing is that some individual temperaments are naturally inclined towards classical values – towards reason, restraint, clarity and balance – and others are inclined towards Romanticism. Some of us are Romantic when young, then take on Classical values as an aspect of maturity. Others come later to Romanticism as a liberation from a restrictive past. Perhaps the best composers embrace something of both, though they may incline in one direction.

The two leading revolutionaries of 20th Century composing were temperamental opposites. Schoenberg was an intense Romantic who had seen all Wagner's main operas around 20 times apiece by the time he was 25. Stravinsky was the Classicist who believed that music, by its very nature, was 'essentially powerless to *express* anything at all'.

Schoenberg's early music was part of the artistic

FROM THE DEPTHS OF TIME

movement of Expressionism, the final, most extreme manifestation of the Romantic movement that wore its raw psyche on its sleeve. It embraced the other arts, particularly cinema and painting. Schoenberg was no bad painter himself, exhibiting with Kandinsky and the *Blaue Reiter* group.

In 1909 Schoenberg wrote ***Erwartung*** (*Expectation*), a harrowing piece for soprano and orchestra in which the music follows the rapid shifts of emotion – from fear to anger to guilt to love – of a woman searching in a forest for her lover. In fact Schoenberg implied that the action covers only a single second in which she finds his corpse, and the music expands that moment over half an hour. ***Erwartung*** has no form in the traditional sense, and its melodies are atonal: they have no relation to any key but seem to follow the dictates of emotional states. Though it was not performed until 1925, it comes straight out of pre-war Vienna, where Freud was laying bare the compulsions and nightmares of the Subconscious.

An equally apocalyptic breakthrough was made in 1913 by the other 20th Century revolutionary. In his ballet ***The Rite of Spring*** Stravinsky now did for rhythm what Schoenberg was doing for melody. In fact rhythm, as compared with harmony, had never really developed very far in Western classical music. Persistent, driving pulses and irregular accents seemed to belong to the practices of faraway savages. In this vision of a pagan sacrificial rite, climaxing with a girl dancing herself to death, there is a frantic rhythmic energy but no consistency of pulse to push the music forward. As a result the music, even when separated from the ballet, has the on-the-spot convulsiveness of a frenetic dance .

It was a very dramatic step that Stravinsky took to liberate conventional pulse in this piece, and like Schoenberg he struck deep into something primitive: a collective unconscious, more Jung than Freud. The first playthrough of the complete work was on two pianos by Stravinsky and Debussy at the home of the journalist Louis Laloy. 'We were dumbfounded,' wrote Laloy, 'flattened by a hurricane from the depths of time…' And that was before the addition of Stravinsky's exhilarating orchestral colouring.

The premiere in 1913 remains one of the great moments in musical history. The uproar and upset showed music to have the power to shake the bedrock of Western civilization.

In fact Stravinsky was a highly civilized man who prized order and precise control. Nevertheless here was a chasm opening in the landscape of Western culture, hinting at untamed monsters below.

Stravinsky, Schoenberg, Freud, Jung. And of course the Great War that was about to really change everything.

1912

Schoenberg *Pierrot Luniere*
Prokofiev *Piano Concerto No.1*
Grainger *Handel in the Strand*
Satie *Trois veritable preludes
flasques (pour un chien)*
Delius *On Hearing the First
Cuckoo in Spring*

Arnold Schoenberg

1874-1951 (left)

Austrian Jew who fled Nazi Europe for the USA.
Inclined towards subject-matter like madness and
violence, though in later life he embraced Jewish
religious themes. Early works (eg. *Verklärte Nacht*)
were intensely romantic and just about tonal.
Pursuing a starker expressionism he found it
necessary to abandon tonality, then felt the weight
of history on him to invent a new framework to
take its place. The result was the twelve-tone
system of 'serialism', which brought him much
ostracism and ridicule but also showed the way
for many other composers during and after his
lifetime. Listeners have been less enthusiastic.

Alexander Zemlinsky

1871-1942

Schoenberg's friend, brother in law and teacher, a
devoted disciple of Mahler (and erstwhile suitor of
Mahler's wife Alma, who called him a gnome). His
rich, late-romantic music was admired by his fellow composers, and his conducting was respected
widely. Persecuted by the Nazis, he fled to the
USA in 1938 and died an unknown.

Charles Ives *1874-1954 (left)*

The father of modern American music, a weekend composer: he ran an insurance firm. Indulged in wide experimentation unhampered by concern for European tradition, for public taste, or indeed for whether his work was performed at all. Thus by 1920 he had, uncannily, anticipated most of the century's new trends. A forthright, pioneering New Englander with a sentimental attachment to hymntunes. Believing most European music was 'goddam sissy' (Mozart: effeminate. Chopin: wore a skirt), he loved good masculine cacophony (as when he heard two marching bands meet head-on, playing different tunes) yet married a woman called Harmony.

Igor Stravinsky *1882-1971*

Composing's Picasso, a celebrity and icon, whose style developed adroitly in line with the fast-changing world around him. Lured by Diaghilev from Russia to Paris in 1910, he wrote the ballet scores *The Firebird*, *Petrushka* and *The Rite of Spring* for the Ballets Russes, then *Pulcinella*, which led the Neo-classical vogue in the 1920s. Despite criticism from modernists that neo-classicism was an artistic retreat, he managed to never quite go out of fashion throughout his long life. In 1939 he emigrated to the USA and became even more of a celebrity when *The Rite of Spring* was used to accompany dinosaurs in Disney's film *Fantasia*. Then he wrong-footed his public once more by taking up serialism late in the day, after years of slagging it off, and after Schoenberg had died.

Karol Szymanowski *1882-1937*

Polish composer and educationalist. Tubercular from childhood, he died from smoking-induced cancer. The family home was destroyed in the Russian Revolution. His heart was to be buried next to Chopin's but War intervened and it was destroyed in the Warsaw Uprising. Also burned was a homosexual novel that he had written. His music, sensual and passionate, fuses Polish folk idioms with a dionysian Catholicism.

Leoš Janáček
1854-1928 (right)

The earliest-born of 20th century composers, a Moravian who hit success in his sixties with his opera *Jenůfa*. Became more inspired the older he got, partly due to pride in the newly-created Czechoslovak Republic and partly to an unreciprocated fixation on a married woman 40 years younger than himself. His music is passionate and incorporates speech patterns and folk idioms.

1916

Bax *The Garden of Fand*
Falla *Nights in the Gardens of Spain*
Holst *The Planets*
Grainger *The Warriors*
Nielsen *Symphony No.4 (Inextinguishable)*

Percy Grainger *1882-1961*

Australian-born concert pianist and experimental composer with huge, chaotic output scored for strange instrumental combinations. Lived in England from 1901 and the USA from 1914. Indulged in folksong collecting and sado-masochism. Eccentric, bordering on bonkers, he travelled with whips in his suitcase, loved stale bread and believed in blue-eyed Aryan superiority. Most of these proclivities originated in his dominating, possessive mother. When she committed suicide he found a Nordic blonde who reminded him of her, and married her during a concert at the Hollywood Bowl (audience: 20,000). Spent his final years attempting to construct a 'free music machine'. Died a marginalised figure, remembered mainly for engaging arrangements of folksongs like *Country Gardens*.

Gustav Holst

1874-1934

Unassuming English composer and trombonist, who might have written much more if he had not also been a school-teacher. Often ill from overwork, asthma and problems with nerves in his arm, he went to an early grave, and is probably continuously turning in it as his suite *The Planets* sustains its huge success. Absolute integrity seems to have prevented him from accepting its status as a modern masterpiece.

A mystic with his feet on the ground, he studied Sanskrit and composed much for his pupils to play (eg *St.Paul's Suite*). His musical language shows a Stravinsky-like fascination with asymmetrical rhythms and ostinato.

Owned Beethoven's tuning fork.

Arnold Bax

1883-1953 (right)

A Romantic, despite being born in Streatham, who loved Irish and Celtic culture (he wrote novels under the pseudonym Dermot O'Byrne). Neither his wife and kids nor his mistress (the pianist Harriet Cohen) could tie him down, and he spent much of his life staying in pubs, composing at battered pianos. As fashion left him behind, he turned increasingly to drink and took an extra (younger) mistress. When World War II began he settled down for life at a pub in Sussex.

CLASSICAL SOLDIER MEETS JAZZ DEVIL

3

Stravinsky wrote **The Soldier's Tale** in 1918 for a small ensemble plus narrator. It was intended to tour easily in difficult times. This Faustian fable of a soldier who makes a pact with the devil contained parodies of tango and ragtime. Stravinsky had not heard ragtime, only seen sheet music brought back from America, but was quick to incorporate it in his works. However it wasn't long before ragtime was overtaken by the arrival in Europe of full-blown jazz.

Classical music cross-fertilised with jazz for the rest of the century. Jazz put a premium on skill and virtuosity. It was also experimental and forward-looking: it was bound to appeal to composers. Orchestral players heard Louis Armstrong and went back to school. Stravinsky licked his lips and knew he could write challenging rhythms that a new generation of orchestral players could be expected to master. But to much of classical music's public, jazz was the Devil's music, with its primitive jungle rhythms and low-life origins. Even the name 'jazz' had some unspecified sexual meaning. And its purveyors were Negros, the sort of people Europeans send missionaries out to. It was a bit disconcerting them bringing their gospel over here.

LAST RAGTIME IN PARIS

By 1919 Debussy had died, the War was over, and Paris had eclipsed Vienna as the artistic place to be. The celebrity list was extraordinary: Picasso, Braque, Hemingway, Gertrude Stein, Joyce, Pound, Stravinsky, Apollinaire, Man Ray, Cocteau. There were American writers escaping Prohibition and enjoying a good exchange rate (until the 1929 Crash); young composers such as Copland, taking lessons from the famous teacher Nadia Boulanger. And the Ballets Russes – though past their prewar heyday – where Diaghilev commissioned new works from composers, to be performed by Nijinski with costumes by Bakst. Satie's 1917 ballet **Parade** was based on a scenario by Cocteau with set designs by Picasso. Milhaud's **La Création du Monde** in 1923 had set designs by Léger and the music was heavily tinged with jazz.

For the moment popular influences predominated: opera was less important than caberet. Revue Négre jazzband, with Sidney Bechet and Josephine Baker, brought Black culture. Cocteau gave poetry readings to a jazz accompaniment.

The War had finished off the Romantic movement. Now music also turned its back on Debussy and Ravel, whose prewar score **Daphnis and Chloé** had seemed to promise that the Impressionist torch would be carried on. 'Enough of clouds, waves and nocturnal scents' proclaimed Cocteau, 'what we need is everyday music'. Music of clarity, simplicity and humour, inspired by fairs, circuses, music hall and cabaret, as well as everyday sounds such as typewriters.

A fairground atmosphere pervades Milhaud's infectious **Le Bœuf Sur le Toit**, a collection of Brazilian dance tunes that move though the full cycle of keys with regular returns of the rollicking rondo theme. The piece, first conceived for a silent film, was turned by Cocteau into a ballet for clowns and was an instant success. It gave its name to Europe's first jazz club, opened in 1922 in the bar in which *Les Six* met regularly. *Bœuf* became jazz slang for a jam session.

Stravinsky had emerged as the pre-eminent composer and having proclaimed the future with **The Rite of Spring** he was now reinventing the past. The new fashion of Neo-classicism really began with **Pulcinella**, his exquisite reworking of early 18th Century pieces attributed to Pergolesi. Prokofiev had written his **Classical Symphony (No.1)** three years earlier, a charming tribute to the time of Haydn, but Stravinsky's quirky orchestration and constant rhythmic reshuffling added an ironic irreverence. Neo-classicism was a form of detachment, an antidote to the intensity of the Expressionists, and its language was new, however familiar the reference point. This distancing was an aim for most 20th Century composers, and Stravinsky in particular.

What did not get played in Paris was the new music of Schoenberg, Webern and Berg. Schoenberg was the enemy in more ways than one, as unpopular as Stravinsky was popular. He may not have minded this, for he thrived on opposition. Looking back later on his achievements he said 'the credit must go to my opponents'. As a traditionalist he understood how hard his work was to listen to, but also that the imperative of history required him to take the steps he did. Already the first to plunge into atonalism, he took the more radical step in 1924 of formulating the twelve-tone system of 'serialism' to replace what was lost when harmony, melody and key were discarded. Tonalism was a hierarchy: there had always been dominating notes in any given key (*doh*, *me*, *soh*), and accidentals (flats and sharps) which were like the peasants in the hierarchy. Atonalism treated all notes as equal; serialism required that they were played in a certain order, to be fixed for each individual composition. Schoenberg's pupils, Berg and Webern, took up serialism enthusiastically. They all got used to outcries and walkouts at their concerts.

In Britain outbreak of war had brought a ban on modern German music in the Prom concerts. Vaughan Williams had already broken from the Elgarian tradition, taking lessons from Ravel and looking to develop French rather than German textures. His **Pastoral Symphony (No.3)**, incubated whilst on war service as an ambulanceman in France, consisted of four slow, contemplative movements in a timeless, modal language. The 'Pastoral' label has done harm to this work which evokes, rather than cows looking over gates, the massive quietness of a wartorn landscape.

Arnold Bax, in contrast, had managed to avoid the fighting, and had used the war years to compose some of his best works, including the seascape

Tintagel. Thus, as other composers returned exhausted from the trenches, he had works ready to establish his pre-eminence in 1920s England. There was a new belief in English music and a feeling of no need to abandon Romanticism or Impressionism, let alone listen to the likes of Schoenberg.

The real frontier of modernism was emerging in New York, where Cowell was requiring pianists to reach into their pianos to pluck the strings. and Varèse was causing uproar with **Hyperprism**, which utilised a siren among the instruments – not for him a symbol of wartime alarm, but an abstract, parabolic sound shape.

Nadia Boulanger
1887-1979

and Lili Boulanger
1893-1918

Composing sisters, educated by their aristocratic Russian mother. Nadia's fame rests on her influence as a remarkable teacher to the likes of Carter, Copland, Berkeley and Glass. She also revived the music of Monteverdi, which had been neglected for some time. Did much to promote the music of her sister Lili, who had composed prolifically throughout her short life despite perpetual illness and was the first woman to win the *Prix de Rome*.

1917

Prokofiev *Symphony No.1*
(Classical)
Bax *Tintagel*
Satie *Parade*
Holst *Hymn of Jesus*
Ireland *Violin Sonata No.2*

(from left) Poulenc, Satie, Milhaud

Les Six

A shortlived Parisian group (founded 1920) comprising four Frenchmen, a Frenchwoman and a Swiss, loosely united by the influence of Cocteau and Satie, and with an inflated reputation for outrageousness.

MILHAUD

Erik Satie
1866-1925

Father figure, but not actually a member of *Les Six*. Considered by Cocteau to be 'the supreme anti-Romantic', an eccentric who, though penniless, owned nine identical grey suits. He composed curiously spare, directionless piano pieces with quirky, rather dadaist names like *True Flabby Preludes (for a dog)*. Played piano in Montmartre's *Black Cat* café, but drank his wages and died of cirrhosis. Never used soap.

Francis Poulenc
1899-1963

Parisian playboy with a private income from pharmaceuticals who professed to have frequented the music hall 'without stop from age 15 to 30'. Took on something of Satie's wit and Stravinsky's detachment. Ill-starred love affairs with younger men and the death of a friend led him to embrace Catholicism in the 1930s. Thereafter his music gained in spiritual profundity, though frivolity was never far away. For some outside France his disconcerting tendency to juxtapose the sacred and the trivial may have obscured his qualities as a fine melodist who wrote particularly well for the voice.

Darius Milhaud
1892-1974

Adventurous Provençal Jewish composer who poured out music of confusing diversity, using polytonality (several keys simultaneously), jazz elements and Brazilian dances encountered in his two-year stay in South America. Took a while to outgrow a reputation for trendiness and clowning following his ballet *Le Bœuf sur le Toit*. Rheumatoid arthritis made him increasingly wheelchairbound.

Les Six continued…

Louis Durey 1888-1979

Soon abandoned *Les Six*, later joining the Progressistes, Communists dedicated to writing music of mass appeal (eg. *La Longue Marche* to a text by Mao)

Germaine Tailleferre

1892-1983 (left)

Changed her name from Taillefesse (*fesse* means buttock). Wrote a lot more than the short, charming Satie-influenced works she was known for in the Twenties. (Cocteau compared her to a watercolourist.) For a while she was married to the caricaturist Ralph Barton. Outlived the rest of *Les Six*, composing into her eighties 'because it amuses me. It is not great music, I know'.

Les Six continued…

Arthur Honegger *1892-1955*

The Swiss one, and only a member of *Les Six* because he was a friend of Poulenc. In fact he was antipathetic to Satie, and unsympathetic to French flippancy. A Romantic who loved Bach, he is best known for his musical depiction of a locomotive *Pacific 231*. World War II left him depressed and hopeless about composing.

Georges Auric *1899-1983 (left)*

Youngest of *Les Six* and the one who administered the last straw that caused Satie to walk out on them all, when he stabbed the great man's famous black umbrella.

Manuel de Falla
1876-1946

Spain's foremost modern composer. His love of Spanish culture and Catholic ritual was combined in his music with the influence of Debussy, absorbed while in Paris from 1907-1914. A neat man, whom Stravinsky called 'as modest and retiring as an oyster'. Though his life was chaste there is sensuousness and passion in his music, which was often too Spanish to French ears and too French to Spanish ears. After the Civil War, distressed particularly by the murder of his friend Lorca, he emigrated to Argentina.

Maurice Ravel
1875-1937

A tiny, fastidious dandy who wrote music of clarity, elegance and wit, meticulously orchestrated. A most civilized composer who respected the past yet embraced contemporary influences like jazz and orientalism. Often underrated as 'the other Impressionist' in Debussy's shadow, he also suffered from going out of fashion after World War I. This was despite being at the height of his powers and writing *Le Tombeau de Couperin* as a tribute to the dead. Best-known for *Boléro*, which he himself dismissed as 'a piece for orchestra without music', and the sumptuous ballet score *Daphnis et Chloé* commissioned by Diaghilev. He kept a picture of his Basque mother (the only woman in his life) above his piano.

1921

Hindemith *Kammermusik*
Vaughan Williams
Symphony No.3 (Pastoral)
Walton *Façade*

Ralph Vaughan Williams
1872-1958 (left)

Darwin's great-nephew, who evolved into a giant of the English music renaissance. He gave tireless encouragement to music-making at every level throughout his long life, yet managed to fit in a considerable body of his own work, including nine symphonies. A role-model for late developers, it was only in his mid-thirties, after taking lessons from Ravel that he found his composing voice, a style enriched by his assimilation of folk and Tudor idioms. The breadth of vision in his music, ranging from the deeply spiritual *Tallis Fantasia* to the violent *Fourth* and *Sixth Symphonies*, is testimony to his humanity. Though an agnostic, he edited the *English Hymnal* writing some of the best-known hymntunes eg. *For All the Saints*.

Frank Bridge
1879-1941

Brighton-born composer, conductor and viola player. Less insular than his English contemporaries, he was not afraid of dissonance (eg. *Third and Fourth String Quartets*). A considerable influence as teacher and mentor to Benjamin Britten.

Anton Webern

1883-1945

Schoenberg's pupil, a serialist of matchless succinctness (total output: three CDs worth). He rarely heard his work performed, but tended each note on the page with precision and refinement, paring down a full range of emotions into something like musical bonsai. The postwar avant-garde took his work as a starting point, but he was not there to hear the results. Having survived being blacklisted by Hitler, he was accidentally shot by an American soldier as he stepped outside to smoke a cigar.

Alban Berg

1885-1935

Another pupil of Schoenberg, though his serialism was shot through with the late-romanticism of Mahler. His music is rich, tense and complex, full of large-scale palindromes and intricate ciphers, and usually inspired by relationships, either amorous or platonic. The *Violin Concerto* is dedicated 'To the Memory of an Angel' who was in fact Mahler's wife's teenage daughter by her second husband. The *Lyric Suite* is full of coded references to his secret mistress, who was Mahler's wife's third husband's sister. Wrote two powerful, expressionist operas, *Wozzeck* and *Lulu*. Always a hypochondriac (he once insisted Freud treat his sore throat), he surprised all his friends by actually dying of an infected wasp sting.

41

Edgard Varèse
1883-1965

Henry Cowell *1897 – 1965 (left)*

Energetic US American experimentalist, who asked pianists to play 'clusters' of notes with their elbows, or directly pluck or brush the strings (as in *Aolian Harp* and *The Banshee*). Invented an instrument called the rhythmicon, and first put the idea of the player-piano into the head of Conlon Nancarrow.

Uncompromising visionary who set out with siren, tape-recorder and sundry electronics to prove that noise could be music. His earlier pieces had been more romantic but were lost in a fire when he left Europe for New York. This move he celebrated with *Amériques*, which one reviewer likened to the progress of a fire through a large zoo. Born before his time, he dreamed of electronic music before the technology was available. Lack of appreciation left him depressed throughout the 1930s and 1940s, but when Le Corbusier designed the Philips pavilion for the World Exhibition of 1958 he arranged for *Poème Électronique* to be blasted out from hundreds of loudspeakers, fulfilling Varese's dream of sound moving through space and time.

George Gershwin
1898-1937

Highly gifted Russian-Jewish-American composer (original name Gershovitz) on the popular/jazz edge of classical. Died at 39 of a brain tumour. Wrote some of the great songs - eg. *Summertime* and *I Got Rhythm*, as well as larger-scale works such as *Rhapsody in Blue* and *An American in Paris*. Inclined to ask other composers for lessons: Stravinsky responded by asking him his income and remarked 'You teach <u>me</u>'.

Béla Bartók *1881-1945 (left)*

Hungary's greatest composer and folk music collector. No-one immersed themselves more thoroughly in the raw materials of folk melody and rhythm and this, along with other influences, helped create his own idiosyncratic musical language. Enjoyed using dissonance and applying to music structural principals like arch forms and the Golden Section. Had a remarkable ear, and often used quarter-tones (notes lying between two halftones), and sounds evocative of insects in his eerie 'night music'. Six string quartets span his creative life; they are sometimes astringent, sometimes rhythmic and exuberant. He was exiled in the USA during World War II, and though ill with leukaemia, rallied with each commission. His style mellowed: *Concerto for Orchestra*, one of the 20th Century's masterpieces of technique and structure, is very accessible, and the final *Piano Concerto No.3* is almost Mozartian.

Zoltán Kodály *1882-1967*

Bartók's collaborator, with Edison phonograph and wax cylinders, in folksong collecting expeditions. Stayed on in Hungary during Nazi occupation and completed their huge compendium of folk music in 1951. His compositions include many fine choral pieces. He believed singing to be the key to musicianship and had much influence on education in Hungary.

IRRESISTIBLE FORCE MEETS IMMOVABLE OBJECTION

The role of the artist in society in times of political instability was the highly pertinent subject of Hindemith's opera **Mathis der Maler***. While Strauss and Orff believed they could serve German music without serving the Nazis, and Weill and Eisler sniffed revolution, Hindemith engaged with the dilemmas of his time. His conclusion seems to have been that the artist was better committed to his art rather than to a Brechtian engagement in politics. But such subtleties cut no ice with Goebbels, for whom Hindemith's modernism simply meant Jewishness: 'His blood may be purely German', he ranted, 'but this only provides drastic confirmation of how deeply the Jewish intellectual infection has eaten into the body of our own people'.*

Soviet composers were also engaged with the tensions between art and politics, arguing out the interpretation of Lenin's dictat that art must unite and inspire the masses. But when Stalin walked out of Shostakovich's opera **Lady Macbeth** *it was after the bit that satirised the police. Likewise, for all Hindemith's philosophising,* **Mathis der Maler** *was banned because it depicted the corruption of power. Dictators can be quite pragmatic about the Arts.*

4

RISE AND FALL

Economic crisis and the rise of dictatorships made the 1930s a very different decade from the 1920s. Music now turned its back on parody and skittishness towards a more direct and serious purpose. Some composers responded to the climate by delving into their religious beliefs. Stravinsky returned to the Russian Orthodox Church and wrote his **Symphony of Psalms**. Schoenberg returned to his Jewish roots and began his prolonged theological and musical struggle to compose **Moses und Aron**. This was a formative time, too, for Messiaen, possibly the most religious composer of the century.

In Germany, **The Rise and Fall of the City of Mahagonny** caused riots with its biting satire on capitalism. A collaboration between composer Kurt Weill and didactic playwright Bertold Brecht – who believed that a new, simple form of people's opera would emerge from 'the coming liquidation of all bourgeoise arts' – it scandalised moral, religious and political sensibilities. The deliberately sleazy, jazz cabaret feel of the music stoked up the atmosphere of decadence. Within three years, Hitler was in power and both Brecht and Weill had fled for the USA. Also packing his suitcase was Paul Hindemith, dismissed from his teaching job by the Nazis and labelled a 'cultural Bolshevik'.

In the USSR, where the real Bolsheviks were, composers had no way of escaping their straitjacketing. The early days of the Revolution had freed up the Arts but with Stalin now in power the newly established Composers' Union dictated that music should shun 'formalism' and inspire optimism. Shostakovich was at that point a progressivist who had dipped into several atonal pots, Berg in particular, while serving the state as he believed he should by remaining an accessible 'realist'. His psychological opera **Lady Macbeth of the Mtsensk District** had been performed very successfully – 83 times in St Petersberg and 97 times in Moscow alone between 1934 and 1936 – when he read in *Pravda* a stinging attack on its 'formalism' and 'bourgeoise sensationalism', and saw the writing on the wall.

Taking formalism to mean almost any 20th Century technique, he withdrew both **Lady Macbeth** and his Mahlerian **Fourth Symphony** (saving his career, perhaps even his life) and began a new one. This **Fifth Symphony** was tuneful and optimistic, and the premiere went well. Maybe this was indeed 'what the people wanted', or perhaps the people were relieved that their best composer was prepared to toe the line. A journalist dubbed it 'a Soviet artist's reply to just criticism' and Shostakovich allowed the tag to stand.

Paul Hindemith
1895-1963

An enfant terrible in 1920s Germany who left home aged eleven to become a busker. After early operas about murder, castration and the sexual fantasies of a nun he settled for a while into neo-Baroque and jazz idioms before joining the Brecht bandwagon with direct, polemical pieces (eg. *Lehrstück)*. Became duller in the USA, but respectable.

Kurt Weill
1900-1950

Jewish Marxist who fused jazz and cabaret with his classical style in what now seems the evocation of 1930s Berlin. Hit fame collaborating with Bertold Brecht in *The Threepenny Opera*, written for the smoky voice of Lotte Lenya, whom he married twice. Fled the Nazis for the USA, where he wrote Broadway musicals, believing them the best way to speak to the Proletariat.

William Walton

1902-1983

Unassuming son of an Oldham choirmaster, adopted by Edith Sitwell and her brothers. Set her poems to music in *Façade*, launching him as a 19-year-old enfant terrible... though not so terrible for long. The 1953 *Coronation March* and film music for Olivier's *Henry V* proved his status, and *Belshazzar's Feast* has become a choral society mainstay, but he found composing tortuous ('My eraser is more important than my pencil') and never recaptured his early verve.

Constant Lambert

1905-1951 (right)

For a while England's leading young composer, writing bright, jazz-influenced music. He wrote *Rio Grande* at 24, taking London by storm. Directed Sadler's Wells Ballet and became Margot Fonteyn's lover. Prone from childhood to illness (he had one lame foot and one deaf ear), he succumbed to heavy drinking and ill-health (including undiagnosed diabetes). His son Kit, who also died young, was manager of *The Who*.

Sergey Prokofiev *1891-1953*

Prolific and precocious Russian composer (wrote his first opera at 9), a combination of astringent modernist and lyrical traditionalist. After the Revolution he left for the USA and Paris, but despite much success (eg. with *Lieutenant Kijé*) returned to the USSR in 1936 just in time for the Stalinist clampdowns on the Arts. He died a few hours before Stalin.

Dmitri Shostakovich

1906-1975

Composing giant of the USSR. His 15 string quartets reveal much introspection and despair while his 15 symphonies, heir to Mahler's in language and narrative scope, tell of his epic battle for creative freedom. His *First Symphony* was written whilst a teenage student, supporting his widowed mother and sisters. Fell foul of Stalin in 1936 and again in 1948 and slept with a bag packed, in perpetual danger of being made an unperson. His music reflects his ambiguous position, with undercurrents of irony and hollowness in its declamatory moments, and Mahlerian juxtaposition of the sublime with the banal. The emotional range, from grotesque humour to searing despair, and his habitual, often perplexing, quotations from his own and others' music, portray a complex as well as brave character.

Carl Orff *1895-1982*

Influential educationalist who believed music was in everybody and was best united with speech and dance in 'total theatre'. Of his own compositions (which Stravinsky dubbed 'neo-Neanderthal'), the rhythmically primal *Carmina Burana* stands out. Composed music for the Olympics in Munich 1972 and, more controversially, in Berlin 1936.

Hanns Eisler

1898 - 1962

Pupil of Schoenberg who became Bertold Brecht's most enduring collaborator. A Communist who managed to be exiled by both Nazi Germany and McCarthyite America. After winning Oscars for the film scores of *None but the Lonely Heart* and Fritz Lang's *Hangmen Also Die* he was deported in 1950 to East Germany, where he wrote the National Anthem.

Samuel Barber *1910-1981*

Unreconstructed Romantic who pierced the heart of the American psyche with his *Adagio for Strings.* Long separated from the string quartet it was originally part of and eclipsing all the other good things he wrote, it is reached for whenever a cathartic expression of grief is needed: the funerals of Einstein and Roosevelt, the film *Platoon* and in the aftermath of the September 11th tragedy. Barber continued to compose in Romantic vein for the rest of his life, unperturbed by changing fashions, and died in the arms of his partner, the composer Menotti.

Aaron Copland

1900-1990

Like Gershwin, an American from Russian emigré stock (original name Kaplan). Studied with Boulanger in 1920s Paris, then returned eager to forge an authentic American classical sound. This he did, taking something from jazz, Shaker hymns and rodeo songs and adding his personal rhythmic vitality and orchestral clarity. His trilogy of *Billy the Kid*, *Rodeo* and *Appalachian Spring* are testimony to his belief in the need to communicate with the public, but eclecticism led him to embrace tougher idioms including serialism. Always relaxed about his homo-sexuality, his lovers included the young Leonard Bernstein.

Joaquin Rodrigo
1901-1999

The most completely 20th century composer (he only missed one year of it). In fact his musical feet were planted firmly in Spain's glorious past. Studied in France, thereby missing the Civil War, then returned to Franco's Spain in 1939 where he scored an immediate and lifelong hit with *Concierto de Aranjuez*. The rest of his work followed the same conservative formula without the star quality and had a suffocating effect on the developments in Spanish music initiated by Falla. Blind from childhood diphtheria, he wrote all his works in braille and was much supported by his wife, a Turkish pianist.

Heitor Villa-Lobos
1887-1959

and Carlos Chávez
1899-1978

Villa-Lobos *(left)* was a larger-than-life, cigar-smoking Brazilian composer who played from boyhood in street bands and cafés in Rio. Probably mastered more instruments than any other composer. He visited Paris in the 1920s, collected indigenous Indian music and inspired a new Brazilian musical nationalism. Wrote vast amounts of ambitious music with exotic instrumentation, some of it even louder than his checked shirts.

Chávez was a Mexican conductor, pianist, teacher, writer and government official, and a composer who combined Aztec elements (he was part-Indian) with modernist influences.

59

PACIFIST PIANIST MEETS CONSCIENTIOUS PAGE-TURNER

5

The immediate post-war mood was not to dwell on the horrors, and certainly not to reflect them in music. Not until 1962 was there a musical memorial that captured the public imagination. Britten's **War Requiem***, commissioned to celebrate the rebuilding of Coventry Cathedral on the bombed-out ruins of the old cathedral widened its scope to reflect broadly on 'the pity of war', using the poetry of World War I poet Wilfred Owen. Another apposite work, Tippett's* **A Child of Our Time** *has endured as a reminder, a piece familiar to all choral singers. It is rooted in real events of 1938 and punctuated by spirituals just as Bach's masses were punctuated by chorales.*

Tippett and Britten met up in curious circumstances in Wormwood Scrubbs Prison. Britten was doing his bit for morale by playing the piano to the inmates. Tippett, who was doing time for conscientious objection, stepped out of the audience to turn the pages.

GRAVE NEW WORLD

Among the many European exiles arriving in the New World around the time of the Second World War were Schoenberg and Stravinsky, who both settled in Hollywood but avoided each other. As a German Jew, Schoenberg had no choice but exile. Stravinsky, whose wife and daughter had died of tuberculosis, wanted a new start. He had many wealthy American admirers.

On arrival, many composers felt they should lighten their style for American taste. Schoenberg returned to tonalism, Weill wrote Broadway musicals. Stravinsky wrote a tango, then found himself a household name when **The Rite of Spring** was used in Disney's film *Fantasia* .

Bartók, a most reluctant exile who intended to return to Hungary but died before he could, wrote some of his most accessible pieces in America, including the work for which he is most remembered, **Concerto for Orchestra**. For Erich Korngold, arriving in America was like a homecoming, and the Hollywood taste for schmaltzy romanticism gave him his chance to win adulation and Oscars. He was the first film composer to receive fan mail, though the occasional critic was unable to resist the phrase 'more corn than gold'.

Back in the Old World, Olivier Messiaen had been incarcerated in a prisoner of war camp in Silesia. Somehow his fellow-prisoners included a cellist, a violinist and a clarinetist, each with his instrument. Using paper and pencil smuggled in by a German officer, Messiaen began composing one of the landmarks of 20th Century Music. *Quartet for the End of Time* refers to the Book of Revelation's vision of the apocalyptic moment when Eternity begins, as well as to the piece's liberation from musical time. To the parts for the three instrumentalists he added a tricky fourth part for himself on a battered piano. The performance, to more than four thousand fellow-prisoners on a bitterly cold day goes down as one of music's most unusual premieres. 'Never have I been listened to with such rapt attention and comprehension,' said Messiaen. It's an extraordinary thought: for so many ordinary human beings to be so moved by a piece of demanding, modern chamber music. 'Beauty is beyond horror,' said Messiaen.

Bohuslav Martinů

1890-1959

Czech violinist and prolific
composer who absorbed
influences of Stravinsky
and jazz while in Paris,
combining them with
Czech folk rhythms and
melodies. Exiled thanks
to Nazis and Communists,
he spent the War years
in the USA. Always carried
a picture postcard of the
view from the church
tower in which he
lived as a child.

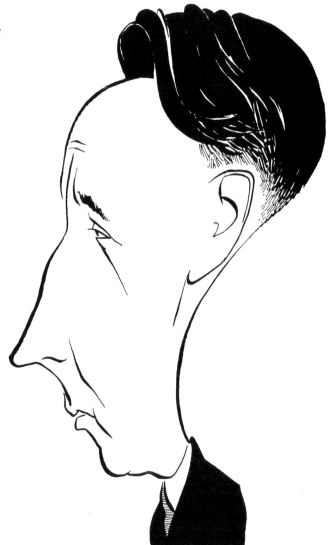

Erich Korngold

1897-1957

Jewish Viennese child prodigy (aged 9
he impressed Mahler with a cantata, at
12 his first ballet was conducted by
Zemlinsky). A Romantic melodist born
rather too late, though just in time to
write music for Hollywood, where he
settled in 1934. Both these factors
doomed him to disdain and neglect
after his return to Vienna in 1949.

Michael Tippett

1905-1998

Erudite English composer whose music expresses his mystical and philosophical concern with human conflicts and ideals. He underwent Jungian analysis, partly to come to terms with his homosexuality. Jungian concepts such as reconciliation of the light and shadow sides recur throughout his work, especially in the oratorio *A Child of Our Time* and his five sophisticated operas. *A Midsummer Marriage* is full of archetypes; *The Knot Garden* features a psychoanalyst with Prospero Complex, and his clients. *The Ice Break* features an androgynous psychedelic messenger called Astron.

Benjamin Britten

1913-1976

A most influential modern
English composer, he com-
posed from the age of five
and had written eleven
piano sonatas by the age
of 13. His style owes
much to his teacher
Frank Bridge and the
17th Century
Englishman Henry
Purcell. He paid
homage to
them both
with
*Variations on
a Theme by
Frank Bridge* and
*The Young Person's Guide to the
Orchestra*. Such orchestral pieces
show him to be a master of dramatic
and atmospheric orchestration, though
most of his music was written to be
sung: often by children but particularly
by the tenor voice of his life partner,
Peter Pears.

65

Luigi Dallapiccola

1904-1975

Italian composer with an understandable preoccupation with themes of persecution and liberty. Studied music in World War I detention camps. His *Canti di Prigionia* (Songs from Captivity) were premiered on the day Mussolini declared war on the USA. His Jewish wife was dismissed from her job when Italy adopted Hitler's anti-Semitic policies and they spent World War II in and out of hiding. Later he wrote an opera called *Il Prigioniero* and a song cycle *Canti di Liberazione*. His wife produced a daughter named Anna-Libera.

Olivier Messiaen

1908-1992

One of the most original and influential
20th century composers, a French
organist, composer and ornithologist
who spent days notating birdsong ('the
true lost face of music') and incorpora-
ting it in his compositions (eg.*Catalogue
d'Oiseaux, Réveil des Oiseaux, Oiseaux
Exotique* etc). He also assimilated
Ancient Greek and Eastern rhythms and
a variety of modes and scales.
Antipathetic to Neoclassical irony, but
deeply inspired by Catholic faith: 'I am
not a theorist, only a believer dazzled
by the infinity of God'. He had pro-
nounced synaesthesia, seeing specific
colours in music. Among his pupils
were Xenakis, Stockhausen and Boulez.

Lennox Berkeley

1903-89

English composer who read philosophy and French literature at Oxford, where he was also the cox of the rowing VIII. Studied music in Paris with Nadia Boulanger, causing him to take on French qualities of elegance and restraint that set him apart from his English contemporaries. His son Michael is also a composer.

Malcolm Arnold
b.1921

English son of a shoemaker who composed with
the insight gained from years as an
orchestral trumpeter. Unfashionable in being a
melodist and a symphonist, he has often been
sidelined and snubbed, most notoriously by the
BBC in the Sixties. His music shows wit and
exuberance (eg. *The Padstow Lifeboat* for brass
band, with its blaring foghorn in D) but also
bleakness (eg. in his *Ninth Symphony*), expressing his private suffering from depression and
alcoholism. His film scores include *The Bridge
on the River Kwai*, for which he got an Oscar.

Elizabeth Maconchy
1907–1994 (left)

Composer of vigorous music with the flavour of
Bartók, including 14 string quartets. Pupil of
Vaughan Williams. Wrote music from infancy, but
arrived aged 16 at London's Royal College from
Ireland having only once heard an orchestra. Did
battle with the male musical establishment and
with tuberculosis: she cured herself of the latter
by living in a shed at the bottom of her garden.
Her daughter Nicola Le Fanu is also a composer.

69

Alan Rawsthorne

1905-1971

Elegant, alcoholic Englishman who became a composer after false starts in dentistry and architecture. Confinement to home with illness as a child left him an unworldly, private person. He was, though, close to Constant Lambert, with a shared attitude to music and alcohol. In 1954 he married Lambert's widow and moved to a cottage near Saffron Waldon with 28 cats.

Elisabeth Lutyens

1906-1983

The mother of English serialism, 'Twelve-tone Lizzie', daughter of Sir Edwin the architect. A combative, bohemian aristo-crat, constantly fighting against fashion and sexism, and juggling music with motherhood. A 'character' in the Fitzrovia pubs, interminable phone-drone and inspiring teacher. Some of her most widely appreciated atonal music was writ-ten for the soundtracks of horror films like *The Skull* and *The Earth Dies Screaming*.

CREATIVITY SEEKS NEW RELEASE

6

Ligeti's inclination to swim against the current was put under considerable pressure as the Communist regime bottled up Hungarian culture, jamming the radios and banning the music of Schoenberg and even much of their national icon, Bartók. While he conformed in his daily work, Ligeti secreted away his more radical ideas for another day. When he escaped after the failed uprising of 1956 and arrived on Stockhausen's doorstep in Cologne, his creativity was able to flow at last.

He then found that the freedoms of the West included Stanley Kubrick's freedom to use several of his pieces without permission in the film 2001 – A Space Odyssey. Eventually MGM settled a modest fee out of court, arguing that the film would bring Ligeti's music to millions.

Disney made the same point to Stravinsky when he took liberties with **The Rite of Spring** in Fantasia. At least Stravinsky had the advantage of his music being the starting point for the filming. Prokofiev too was lucky that a good director, Eisenstein, filmed the Battle on Ice sequence in the 1938 film Alexander Nevsky to fit the music as written. But more often film music has been a substance to be edited like everything else in film-making. As Vaughan Williams remarked, 'If you write music for films, you must be prepared to have your head cut off, your tail cut off, even your entrails taken out, and you still must make musical sense'.

In Hollywood, film work provided an income for the new immigrant composers, though it was often a poisoned cup. Most of Korngold's excellent film music was damned by association with poor films. Yet by the end of the century, good films were elevating poor music to concert hall status.

One immigrant who did not get the Hollywood film work he would have liked was the uncompromising Schoenberg. In fact serialism very rarely made it onto the screen. The first time seems to have been in a Tom and Jerry cartoon. And the second time was in a film called The Cobweb, about diseased brains.

NO PAST, NO PERSONALITY

The pendulum swing away from Romanticism reached it's furthest point in the 1950s and 1960s. The reaction was most extreme in countries where extreme things had happened, or where composers' own lives had suffered in extreme ways. There was a strong desire to forget the past and start afresh, and this was keenest in Germany. Summer schools in the small town of Darmstadt became the ideological epicentre for a new progressive movement which brought fresh attitudes into classical music.

Stockhausen and Boulez were the main figures of this movement, and if Schoenberg was a musical Marx with his belief in historical inevitability, these two were music's Stalinists. They saw themselves as leading an avant-garde which was marching in the only legitimate direction for the development of music. Stockhausen believed that 'by the mid-Seventies no-one will listen to Bach or the classics any more'. Other composers were dazzled by his ideas and techniques, his constant experimentation. He and Boulez chose Webern as the starting-point for their 'Year Zero' approach because he was untainted, as they saw it, by Romanticism (unlike Schoenberg). But now they applied his serialism not just to the pitches of notes but to other parameters like rhythm and loudness. Composers were to be architects in sound.

Alongside this urge to obliterate the past was a desire to purge music of individual personality. A system like serialism encouraged this, as did the arrival of electronics. And while Boulez was constructing the perfect system to do the composer's job without involving his personality, so the West Coast Zen Buddhist guru of 'non-intention', John Cage, was aiming at the same goal by employing the element of chance. His mission was to 'let sounds be themselves in space and time'. Composing his **Music of Changes** he made musical decisions in response to the coin-tossing procedures of the *I-ching*. In the notorious **4'33"** the performer played nothing but the audience kept listening, so the 'music' consisted of any extraneous sound they heard.

Understandably, listeners began to feel they were being taken for a ride, particularly when it became clear that the Arts Establishment was supporting the avant-garde in the belief that modern was hip whether you understood it or not. There was much talk of the Emperor's New Clothes. Boulez was unrepentant. 'If you are really creative, and you want to express what you wish to express, I don't think that you can have an audience in mind.' In 1977 the French government gave him a huge grant to establish IRCAM, a hi-tech musical playground under the Pompidou Centre.

Schoenberg had had to fight his battles without that sort of help, as have iconoclastic figures throughout musical history. The implication of establishment support was that doubting listeners were wrong. Whatever the intentions, the result was a wider gulf between composers and their public.

1952

Stockhausen *Kontra-Punkte*
Cage *4'33"*

John Cage
1912-1992

'He's not a composer, he's an inventor – of genius' said Schoenberg about his pupil Cage, the influential American Zen philosopher and mushroom expert (he won $6,000 answering questions on funghi on a quiz show). Believing harmony to be unimportant, and not blessed with much of an ear for it anyway, he concentrated on percussion. Invented the 'prepared piano' by placing various objects between the strings. An explorer of concepts in music such as disconnection and chance, he redefined music as 'organisation of sound' and asked for a new approach to listening: '…not an attempt to understand something that is being said… just an attention to the activity of sounds'. His biggest challenge to listeners was the composition *4'33"* consisting of silence.

Karlheinz Stockhausen

b.1928

Guru and icon of modernity, particularly in
the 1960s, but less so by the 1990s.
Theorist of sound and acoustics, arti-
culator of such concepts as
'moments', 'sound-collectives'
and 'serialised parameters'.
Much of the actual music-
making he left up to the performer, and to chance. A
war orphan from Cologne
who played jazz for the
GIs to finance his music
and philosophy educa-
tion. Became a master of
electronics and sampling
techniques. Hugely
influential – musicians
from Adams to Zappa owe
something to him. Drawn
to the all-embracing potential
of music, he wrote *Gruppen* for
three simultaneously playing
orchestras, and in 1977 began the
seven-part opera *Licht* which may yet
make small fry of Wagner's *Ring*.

Iannis Xenakis
1922 – 2001

Greek composer who trained in engineering. He was wounded, losing the sight in one eye, fighting for the resistance in the 1947 Civil War. Captured and condemned to death, he escaped to France where he took lessons from Messiaen. Worked for the architect Le Corbusier whilst gradually establishing himself as a composer. Applied architectural, mathematical and statistical principles to his music.

Pierre Boulez
b.1925

French composer and pontificating leader of the post-war avant-garde. A gifted mathematician, he was attracted to Webern's strict serialism and took lessons from Messiaen. His music is rigorously intellectual, and sensuous without being remotely emotional. After early successes eg. *Le Marteau sans Maître*, his ability to finish anything to his own satisfaction seems to have gradually waned, along with the whole avant-garde concept. He is, however, a first rate conductor with an acute ear.

Elliott Carter *b.1908*

'Post-avant-garde' American, destined for the family lace import business, but set on composing from the moment he heard *The Rite of Spring*. His parents objected strongly, especially when they found that the man who sold them insurance, that nice Mr Ives, was encouraging young Elliott. He took on board Ives's love of elemental clashes and composed some of the most complex, multi-layered music ever heard. Championed by *The Grateful Dead*, who sponsored a performance and recording of his *Concerto for Orchestra*.

Leonard Bernstein
1918-1990 (right)

Major musical personality, a brilliant, some say overemotional conductor, versatile pianist, rabbinical educator and (his preference) a composer of classical music coloured with jazz. His music for *West Side Story* may yet be considered superior to anything produced by any other US American composer, including many who sneered at his populism and infectious enthusiasm. Chain-smoking got him in the end.

Krzysztof Penderecki
b.1933

Polish composer whose music in the 1960s included the sounds of type-writers, rustling paper, sawing wood, knocking, hissing and whistling. His *Threnody for the Victims of Hiroshima* was one of the most violent and sensational pieces of the avant-garde, as befits its subject. Then, in the 1970s, he came over all romantic.

György Kurtág *b.1926*

Ligeti's friend who assigned opus numbers to his work only after leaving Communist Hungary for Paris. Multilingual and literary, he set texts by Sappho, Kafka and Beckett. A serious, spartan man of few words – and of few notes: he defined for himself tight limits to purge his music of empty gestures. 'One note is almost enough', he claimed – and often one instrument, eg. *Jelek (Signs)* op 5 for viola.

György Ligeti *b. 1923*

Hungarian Jew whose father and brother died in Auschwitz. He fled the ensuing Communist regime in 1956. Musically a complete original, though he embraced some of the avant-garde ideas espoused at Darmstadt. Stockhausen's enthusiasm for electronics fed his inclination towards new textures and micropolyphony (a dense, shimmering flow of sound with no pulse or harmony, memorably associated with the appearance of the monolith in the film *2001*). These static sounds he often contrasts with manic, pulsing activity – a 'clocks-and-clouds' approach. He has a Carrollian sense of the absurd: perhaps the only composer to write a symphonic poem for 100 metronomes.

1963
Feldman *De Kooning*

1964
Riley *In C*

Morton Feldman
1926-1987

Bronx Jew who, after studies with Wolpe that consisted of arguments about music, met Cage, who encouraged him to follow his intuition. This he has done probably more than any composer, working from moment to moment in a piece, with no discernable structural theory. His close friends included the artists Rothko, De Kooning and Pollock, and he himself was the nearest to a painter of any composer. In his music for the *Rothko Chapel*, soft timbres echo the blurred tones of the paintings hung in that Texan sanctuary. Mostly his pieces have no sense of beginning nor end nor direction nor intention, but are sparse brushstrokes of sound mixed with silences . They demand a heightened form of listening, a contemplation, as of ripples on a lake, which can be very rewarding. In the late 1970s his pieces began to expand in length (eg. the five-and-a-half-hour bladder-challenging *String Quartet No.2*).

Stefan Wolpe

1902-1972 (above)

German composer who arrived in the USA in 1938. Studied with Webern and taught at Darmstadt. Otherwise his only vice was chocolate.

Terry Riley

b.1935 (right)

Founding father of Minimalism with his seminal piece *In C*. A groovy laid-back hippie who was a disciple of Indian vocalist Pandit Pran Nath, embraced many influences and influenced many musicians, from Steve Reich to Pete Townshend.

Hans Werner Henze *b.1926*

Prolific German composer whose music encompasses many approaches and ideas, though in the traditional forms of symphonies (nine so far), operas (eg. *The Bassarids*, a reworking of Euripides) and string quartets. Grew up with Nazism and ended the war a British prisoner. Disillusion with both pre- and post-war Germany led him to settle in Italy and embrace the idea of world revolution. In 1968 he became a Marxist, announcing in a tract that his music would now be 'revolutionary' (ie. more easily understood).

Luciano Berio

b.1925

Italian composing magpie with a fascination for theatricality, electronic music, also for language and the voice. In particular the expressive and acrobatic voice of his wife, American singer Cathy Berberian. (eg. in *Recital I*, expressing a psychotic breakdown). Partial to musical collage: *Sinfonia* contains a whole movement of musical quotes from several composers and verbal quotes from Beckett, built around a skeletal rejig of the scherzo from Mahler's *Second Symphony*. At regular intervals from 1958 onwards he wrote *Sequenzas*, virtuoso solo pieces for various instruments including voice.

Witold Lutoslawski
1913-1994

Polish pianist who survived the war by playing in Warsaw cafés. After his *Symphony No.1* (1947) was banned for formalism, he toed the Communist Party line writing folk-based music (the Bartók-influenced *Concerto for Orchestra* was found acceptable). As constraints relaxed in the post-Stalin thaw he heard Cage's music on the radio and began experimenting with radical approaches such as chance.

Andrzej Panufnik
1914-92 (right)

Polish composer of colourful, atmospheric music who also survived the war by playing in Warsaw cafés, sometimes with Lutoslawski. A lover of Mozart and the natural geometry in music, he left Poland for Britain, where he eventually became *Sir* Andrzej. His daughter Roxanna is also a composer.

Henri Dutilleux

b.1916

Fastidious Frenchman whose self-criti-
cism has constrained the size of his output and, perhaps, his reputation. Rich
in colour and orchestration, his music
has a flowing, improvisatory quality.

CACOPHONY MEETS LOST CHORD

⑦ SUPERMARKET

'I was a poor student, so I only had two tape recorders,' says Terry Riley, the grand old man of Minimalism. Like many a musician who had heard Stockhausen, he wanted to play with electronics and repeated patterns. But he was a man with a tonal heart in an atonal decade. In 1964 Riley wrote **In C**, in which players are given 53 tune fragments, each of which they can repeat as many times as they want before moving on to the next loop of sound. Even Schoenberg, the man who had led the plunge into atonalism, insisted that there was 'still much good music to be written in C major.' By the end of the century many composers were back in tonal territory again and, as is the way of pendulum swings, some compositions with the label 'Minimalist' were now so insistently in one key that you ached for a bit of dissonance, or at least a modulation or two.

88

OF SOUND

Listening to Takemitsu in 1999 was not so dissimilar to listening to Debussy in 1900: the consistent feature of music throughout the century was that it was fundamentally static. Whereas 19th Century music was narrative, like literature, 20th Century music was like painting. It needed a new way of listening that required the appreciation of colour and texture, and the sensual qualities of sound for its own sake, rather than following a musical development.

Not everybody hears colour and texture in music, though perhaps many could learn to if they realised it was a good idea. No previous music offers so much of these qualities as do 20th Century compositions. But rather than welcome that gain, we spent the century mourning the loss of melody. Things we can sing or whistle. Even Schoenberg longed for a day when 'people should know my tunes and whistle them'. Webern imagined that in fifty years children would understand his music and sing it. He was very wrong. The 20th Century composers who get their tunes whistled have more often than not been those who to some extent embraced popular music.

When Leonard Bernstein wrote the score for the musical **West Side Story** in the mid-Fifties, the fault-line which he stood astride, between classical and popular music, was beginning to crack wide open. In the years that followed he persisted in his conviction – voiced in his regular educational *Young People's Concerts* on American television – that music was for all the people, and rooted in a tonal language that was universal. He came under heavy fire from the new avant-garde composers to whom the idea of polluting classical music with popular idioms was morally unthinkable.

But… Boulez or Beatles? For the listeners there was just no contest. By the end of the century it was clear it wasn't a question of youth versus age, either. Teenagers didn't grow out of Elvis and discover Elliott Carter. This was the greatest schism in Western music since the Reformation. Classical music has been marginalised ever since, dismissed as irrelevant and elitist .

Yet the final generation of 20th Century composers have grown up comfortable with the idea of integrating within their work influences from both Western popular culture and other ethnic cultures. The breadth and depth of cultural comprehension in people like Reich, Weir, Tavener and Maxwell Davies is unparalleled.

In Japan, Takemitsu grew up enthusiatically absorbing Western pop music alongside classical and jazz. He made arrangements of Beatles songs. Then he was turned on to the Japanese traditional culture in front of his nose through John Cage's interest in it. Such is the musical supermarket at the end of the 20th Century. The success of *Late Junction* on BBC Radio 3 says it all. Every weeknight since 1999 we have been presented with a huge variety of brands of music from any country in the world and any time in history: classical, jazz, folk, ethnic, electronic, new-age, and any fusion of two or more of the above. Classical music's cherished idea of a river of development has split into a delta and arrived at a sea.

Toru Takemitsu
1930-1996

Tiny Japanese composer, the musical equivalent of an abstract landscape painter, rendering into music 'the streams of sounds which penetrate our surroundings'. Bedridden for years as a child, he heard Western classical music and jazz on American forces radio and learned to compose from listening to Duke Ellington, Messiaen, Debussy, Webern, Cage and others, including much pop music. After World War II he gradually opened himself to Japanese traditional culture and allowed Japanese sensibility – and instruments like the biwa and shakuhachi – into his work. Nature is a constant theme, particularly wind and rain. Also formal gardens. He compared writing and listening to music to a walk through a garden. In *Arc*, he says, the orchestra represents rocks, trees, grass etc, and the piano walks though the garden in Part 1, returning along the same path in Part 2. An ardent film buff, he wrote 93 film scores, as well as around 20 books including a detective novel.

Alfred Schnittke
1934-1998 (right)

Russian composer, (parents German and German/Jewish), the epitome of the fin-de-siècle eclectic postmodernist, mixing a broth of musical ingredients with irony and wit. *Symphony No.1* for example 'contains everything that I have ever had or done in my life, even the bad and kitschy as well as the most sincere…' Worldwide appreciation has come with the end of the Cold War.

George Benjamin *b.1960*

Turned on to classical music by Disney's *Fantasia*. Then, after studying with Messiaen from 14, he became at 20 the youngest person to have a work in the Proms: *Ringed by the Flat Horizon* based on part of TS Eliot's *The Wasteland*. The sensual and poetic use of instrumental colours in this and the works of the early 1980s that followed it promised that a direct heir to Debussy and Messiaen had arrived, albeit on the wrong side of the Channel. Since then he seems to have gone rather quiet.

Harrison Birtwistle
b.1934 (right)

Accrington-born member of the 'Manchester school' with Maxwell Davies and Goehr. Though a quiet man, his music is invariably noisy, and he has attracted his own special group of (equally noisy) hecklers. His work has an elemental quality: *Punch and Judy*, for example raised a puppet-show subject to the level of Greek Tragedy, with stylised visceral savagery. Benjamin Britten was one of those who walked out of the premiere.

Peter Maxwell Davies

b.1934 (right)

A composer from the moment, aged four, he heard the Gilbert & Sullivan operetta *Gondoliers*. Interest in serialism gave way to a deeper fascination with the English past, particularly medieval music and history. Enthusiastic and versatile, an anti-elitist campaigner for arts and other issues. Settled in the Orkney Isles since 1970, where he has often collaborated with local writer George Mackay Brown (in eg. *Black Pentecost*, a response to the threat of uranium mining in Orkney)

Arvo Pärt *b.1935 (left)*

Estonian composer who fell foul of the Communist authorities first with early serialist experiments, then with religious music. Escaped to Vienna, then Berlin and has become one of the most frequently performed living composers. His mature style combines the hypnotic effects of Minimalism with elements of ancient religious mysticism. The result is a timeless, contemplative form of music, pared down to simple elements (most characteristically the triad), an approach he refers to as tintinnabulism.

John Tavener *b.1944*

English composer, once associated with the Beatles when he became groovy in the Sixties with his cantata *The Whale.* Weighed down subsequently by the pressures of expectation, he joined the Russian Orthodox Church and changed his style to eastern inspired mystic simplicity. Music to him is a form of prayer, 'iconic', ie. static, simply formed but spiritually profound. The funeral of the iconic Princess Diana proved the ideal occasion to play his *Song for Athene.*

Conlon Nancarrow *1912-1997*

American Communist who worked his passage to Europe playing jazz trumpet. Returning to the USA after fighting against Franco in the Spanish Civil War he had his passport revoked, so from 1940 he settled in Mexico. Here, in years of artistic isolation he made his own music for player-piano (pianola), by punching thousands of holes in the paper rolls. This remarkable music he referred to as 'post-performer' ie. totally impossible for human beings to play. In the 1980s his seclusion was gradually broken as more and more other musicians became aware of him. Ligeti, for example found his music 'perfectly constructed but at the same time emotional… the best of any composer living today'.

Astor Piazzola *1921-1992*

Argentinian composer who spent most of his life playing in tango bands and writing sophisticated tango compositions. Given a bandoneon at the age of eight, he made his first record aged ten. At one point in 1949 he turned his back on the tango in the hope of becoming a more 'serious' composer. Took lessons in Paris with Nadia Boulanger who persuaded him that he and the tango were made for each other. So he went back to writing and playing tangos.

Steve Reich *b.1936 (left)*

American minimalist, a drummer and philosophy graduate
with eclectic musical interests. His early music, eg. *Come
Out* (1966), used identical tape loops played simultaneously but at slightly different speeds, moving gradually
out of phase with each other and creating many varied
patterns and strange acoustic effects before arriving in
phase again. He replicated this approach with musicians (usually taking part himself), starting with
Piano Phase (1967). By the mid-70s he had a cult
following. Subsequent projects became more ambitious, complex and multimedia, often adopting
political subject matter.

Philip Glass *b.1937*

The most interviewed modern composer, with added
potential for punning headlines. Possibly the richest and
most famous living composer too. A Lithuanian-American-
Jewish Minimalist who studied with Milhaud and Boulanger.
From sitarist Ravi Shankar he learned how music could be given
its structure by rhythm. Back in the USA he worked and performed
for a while with Riley and Reich before going his own way with the
specially formed Philip Glass Ensemble and achieving success that
spanned the musical spectrum. With theatre conceptualist Robert
Wilson he produced *Einstein on the Beach*, his first of several operas,
showing him to have an epic and theatrical vision.

Michael Nyman

b.1944

Very successful and versatile composer, notably of music for Peter Greenaway films like *The Draughtsman's Contract*. Erstwhile musicologist, critic and collector of Romanian folksongs, and first (in *The Spectator* in 1968) to utter the word 'Minimalism'. Works include the stage piece *The Man who Mistook his Wife for a Hat* based on a case study by neurologist Oliver Sacks. Also many pieces for the Michael Nyman Band, an idiosyncratic line-up including sackbuts, rebecs and shawms alongside banjo and saxophone, with Nyman on piano.

John Adams

b.1947

The most frequently performed American composer at the century's end. Has made operas out of news stories, most famously *Nixon in China* and *The Death of Klinghoffer* (about the hijacking of the liner *Achille Lauro* and murder of a Jewish passenger). Believing that 'tonality is a natural force, like gravity', he has used Minimalist techniques but with more drama and thrust than his co-Minimalists .

John Adams flanked by Mao Tse-Tung and Nixon

Richard Rodney Bennett *b.1936 (far left)*

Schoolboy protegé of Elisabeth Lutyens, though they fell out violently, then Boulez's first pupil. Has lived in New York since 1979. Effortlessly talented jazz pianist and composer, particularly of music for films eg. *Murder on the Orient Express*. He has dismissed it as journalism: 'one is using a very small part of one's creative ability'.

Robin Holloway *b.1943 (left)*

English composer who, without totally ignoring things going on elsewhere, has fought an unfashionable battle to 'keep a continuity of language and expressive intention with the classics and romantics of the past.'

Oliver Knussen *b.1952 (right)*

Child prodigy son of a double bassist, much in demand as a conductor of 20th-century work, but in his spare moments composer of (eg.) the operas *Where the Wild Things Are* and *Higgledy Piggledy Pop!* based on Maurice Sendak's children's stories.

JOHN MINNION after MAURICE SENDAK

Robert Saxton
b.1953

English Jewish composer of vividly coloured music, a pupil of Elisabeth Lutyens. Works include a *Cello Concerto* for Rostropovich and pieces for his partner, soprano Teresa Cahill. He has written music from the age of six and was the composer featured on BBC Radio 3 at the moment the century ended, though he had not quite met his deadline for *The Wandering Jew*, a Millennium opera for radio. A highly qualified academic (graduate of Oxford and Cambridge) and teacher whose composition pupils have included rising star Thomas Adès.

Judith Weir

b.1954

Possibly Britain's most successful female composer ever, with a knack for clear and direct communication making her popular with audiences and critics alike. She admires folk music for its ability to be very expressive with economical means. After studying with Tavener and Holloway – teachers a world away from the serialist avant-garde – she has produced a series of strong, theatrical pieces. *The Vanishing Bridegroom* shows her fascination with the Gaelic culture of her native Scotland, and she is also able to think herself and her music into other times and other cultures. After her first success, *A Night at the Chinese Opera* (writing her own libretto from a 13th Century Chinese play), she has revisited medieval Spanish legend (*Missa del Cid*), 11th Century warfare (*King Harald's Saga*), and 13th Century Paris (*Lovers, Learners and Libations*).

Mark-Anthony Turnage *b.1960 (left)*

Essex man with a flair for theatrical music and a love of jazz which permeates his work. His orchestral writing has emotional directness and visceral intensity. Operas include *Greek*, a brutal translation of the Oedipus myth into Thatcher's Britain, also *Three Screaming Popes* and *Blood on the Floor*, both based on Francis Bacon's paintings. Much of the latter work was a response to his brother's death from a heroin overdose.

James MacMillan *b.1959*

Scottish composer with a direct, vernacular style steeped in Catholicism that seems unexpected in the last decade of the century. Most of his work has dark undertones which he puts down to the weather. Wrote and conducted the fanfare that launched the Scottish Parliament, and has been outspoken about Scottish chauvinism and anti-Catholic prejudice. Wrote *A Child's Prayer* for choir and two treble soloists in response to the 1996 Dunblane tragedy and a percussion concerto *Veni, Veni Emmanuel* for Evelyn Glennie.

EDWARDIAN SPIRIT MEETS ELABORATING SCRIBE

In the first decade of the 20th Century Vaughan Williams wrote his **Fantasia on a Theme by Thomas Tallis** and shared with listeners his reverence for the music of a long-distant past, expressed in the natural language of 1910. Composers spent much of the century reacting to the past, sometimes rejecting it, sometimes embracing it. In the last decade, Anthony Payne turned his attention back to the 1930s and

finished the symphony Elgar was too old or too dispirited to finish himself, in the language he believed Elgar would have employed. The overwhelming response was of gratitude from listeners who respected the creativity of both composers. But underlying the welcome for Elgar's **Third Symphony** was a feeling of relief from a public who had never worked out how to engage with the changes in musical aesthetics over the 20th Century, and who would not expect to be listening to Anthony Payne's other work. Nor would they have liked it so much if, like Vaughan Williams, Payne had used his own language to convey the other composer's message.

The fact is that, thanks to the recording revolution, most of us spent the 20th Century listening to music from earlier times. Of course it has been a privilege to be transported effortlessly back into the musical souls of Beethoven, Mozart, Bach, Tallis, Hildegard of Bingen. But have we reduced classical music to a dead artefact existing in the present only as archaeology?

This really is up to us because the consumer is now unassailable. The great achievements in art have always been made on the artist's terms, for us to learn to appreciate. No music delivers the full spectrum of emotional, intellectual, sensual and spiritual reward as classical music does, but it comes with a challenge. If we opt out, and reduce listening to passive and comfortable consumerism, the great composer is certain to be a thing of the past.

Anthony Payne *b.1936*

The man who, after many years as a composer in his own right, has gone down in history for his completion (or 'elaboration' as it was coyly called at first), from the sketches Elgar left, of his *Third Symphony*. Though some accused him of 'feasting off the corpse' the result was a triumph, possibly the most eagerly awaited first performance in the last half of the 20th Century .

INDEX
OF CARICATURES

ACKNOWLEDGEMENTS

In researching the text I consulted a number of books the most useful and enjoyable of which I list here. Any factual errors probably came from the web. Sorry, but that's the 21st Century for you.

Paul Griffiths ● *A Concise History of Modern Music*
Michael Hall ● *Leaving Home*
Terry Hiscock ● *Composing Mortals*
ed. Michael Oliver ● *Settling the Score*
Fritz Spiegl ● *The Lives, Wives and Loves of the Great Composers*
ed. Joe Staines ● *The Rough Guide to Classical Music*
John Stanley ● *Classical Music*
● *Wordsworth Dictionary of Musical Quotations*